I0743645

He's Behind You
Just A Little Crush

Elouise East

Copyright © 2020 Elouise East

HE'S BEHIND YOU (JUST A LITTLE CRUSH)

ALL RIGHTS RESERVED

No part of this book may be reproduced or transmitted in any form or by any means, electronic or mechanical including photocopying, recording, or by any information storage or retrieval system, without permission in writing from the publisher, Elouise East. No part of this book may be scanned, uploaded or distributed via the internet or by any other means, electronic or print, without premising from Elouise East.

The unauthorised reproduction or distribution of this copyrighted work is illegal. Please purchase only authorised electronic or print editions and do not participate in or encourage the electronic piracy of copyrighted material. Your support of the author's rights and livelihood is appreciated.

This is a work of fiction. Names, characters, places and incidents are either the product of the author's imagination or are used fictitiously and any resemblance to any actual persons, living or dead, events, or locales is entirely coincidental.

All products and/or brand names mentioned are registered trademarks of their respective holders/companies.

Publisher: Elouise East

Cover Design: Covers by Jo

Editor: Maria Vickers

Beta Readers: Emma Brown, Lisa Kemp

Contents

1

Declan

Declan Scott gulped half a bottle of water before pulling away, gasping for breath. He used his towel to wipe at the sweat coating his face and neck and tried to regain control of his breathing. Damn, he was getting old. He glanced across at the other dancers and actors, seeing them fresh-faced and bushy-tailed, whereas he was a mess.

"Cheer up, Santa. Rehearsal is almost over." Micah Tanner grinned as he slapped Declan on the back.

"Fuck off, Micah," he griped good-naturedly, drinking some more. "Just because you've got fifteen years on me doesn't mean I can't take it."

"Hell no, Declan. You've probably taken part in more pantomimes than all of us put together." Micah waved his hand around, indicating the other members.

"You're digging yourself a hole." He narrowed his eyes. He knew Micah wasn't being unkind; Declan only wanted to mess with him a bit.

"No! Jesus, Declan. You're amazing, is what I'm trying to say." Cheeks flushed, he rubbed the back of his neck.

Declan pushed down the giddiness he felt at the praise and shoved Micah's shoulder, grinning. "Aww, that's so sweet," he replied in a high-pitched voice.

They laughed, as did some of the people close by who'd been listening to their interaction. Declan had seen many members come and go through his twenty-seven years of panto at the Cambridge Theatre. He had started acting in drama plays when he was at school, having caught the bug early. Singing, dancing and acting had not been considered the done thing for a boy when he was at school, but he hadn't cared what anybody said. Still didn't.

Once he'd reach secondary school, the drama classes continued, but he'd added on after school classes, too, both through his school and through a drama company. His first pantomime gig had come about when he'd been enquiring at the theatre for any open positions. The receptionist ushered him back to meet with the manager, who had hired him on the spot. He'd been eighteen at the time and had never looked back.

Returning to the present, Declan studied the people around him, new and old, knowing he didn't have much more time left in him. He was only forty-five, but in pantomime terms, he was ageing out.

"Are you joining us tomorrow night?" Micah broke into his thoughts, and Declan's gaze swung to those piercing green eyes, getting lost before realising he needed to answer the question.

Declan swallowed and nodded. "Yep, wouldn't miss it."

Pantomime season was about to start, and the troupe usually spent one evening the weekend before to let their hair down and relax before the whole routine began. Having one or two performances a day for seven weeks could take its toll. Even with days off and alternating actors, it was a tension-filled, exhausting time.

And Declan wouldn't change it for the world. Although maybe he'd tone down the Christmas decorations and music.

"Great. Maybe we can get your two left feet to relax." Micah danced away as Declan took a swipe at him.

"I'll give you two left feet, asswipe." Declan shook his head, chuckling. He loved the banter they had, something he'd not had so easily with another younger person before.

"Time!"

The choreographer called them back to the stage to begin the next part of the dance sequence. Micah was right about one thing...Declan seemed to have two left feet in the middle part of the last section. He had no idea why, but he kept landing on the wrong foot. It was beginning to piss him off. Putting it out of his mind for the moment, Declan returned his attention to the co-ordinator and took his place, ignoring the way the lights hit the tinsel as it rustled in the air conditioning, flicking red and gold beams in his eyes.

• • • ● ●• ● ● ● • •

The steam rose from the bathwater, and the warmth felt so good against Declan's skin. His muscles ached fiercely, his back twinged, and his head pounded. It wasn't always like this for him, but this week was always the worst. Every year, he joined the rest of the troupe for vigorous training to ensure they had the dance routines and every part of the show running like clockwork. It meant a week's worth of aches and pains, which he had a week to get over before the actual performances began.

He was luckier than most because he didn't have an additional job on top of the pantomime. Throughout his career, he had been in various theatre productions up and down the country, and he'd been able to pay his bills with those jobs. He knew things would be winding down now, so he needed to start thinking about what he could do once he was no longer in the theatre business.

It was a sad thought, and one he didn't want to dwell on too much.

Closing his eyes, he let the heat of the water seep into his muscles. Maybe he needed to get laid. His thoughts flicked to Micah, his heart rate increasing, and he studiously redirected his attention. He tried to think of when the last time he'd slept with someone was but couldn't. That didn't bode well. He might be able to find a nice woman the following night. He was known around Cambridge, so hopefully, he'd have some luck.

After relaxing until the water went cold, Declan drained the bath and dried off. It was early, but he was an early riser, so he decided to go to bed. He grabbed himself a quick drink to rehydrate, then dropped onto his bed, barely able to pull the covers over him before he was asleep.

• • • ● ● • ● • • •

The following evening, Declan checked his appearance in the mirror before heading out the door. He wore his most comfortable—in other words, worn and loose—black faded jeans, an open-collar dark-blue shirt and his trusty leather jacket. Basically, his usual outfit, although a little smarter. His goatee had been trimmed, and the rest of his jaw clean-shaven. If he wanted to find a woman, he needed to look the part.

A wallet, phone and his keys fitted nicely in his pockets, and he heard the taxi beep as he jogged down the stairs, feeling small twinges from the previous week's workouts.

Sliding into the back of the taxi, he settled in for the journey. He'd already booked a taxi home for midnight per his usual routine. He didn't want people seeing him turning into a pumpkin after all. Studying the scenery, he smiled at the thought. It would have been the perfect analogy if they'd been doing Cinderella this year, but they were doing The Snowman instead.

It would be the first time in all Declan's years that they had attempted this. In particular, it had been difficult for the writers to know what to get the characters to say. With the original film being shown mainly with instrumental music, it may have been easier to make it a musical dance show instead of a pantomime, but the writers had managed it. Declan had been pleasantly surprised when he'd read the script.

Best of all, Declan got to play the part of Father Christmas, which he loved. He'd done a few stints over the years of playing Santa at fairs or in stores who wanted someone to talk to the kids for a short time. The children were wonderful. It was part of the reason why Declan hadn't moved into other kinds of acting. Stage performances, for him at least, gave some opportunities for actors to interact with the audience, especially pantomimes, and Declan loved that aspect of it.

One day, he'd love to have kids of his own. He needed to find someone who wanted to settle down before it was too late for him to father them.

Christmas was already in full swing, being mid-November. Decorations were all over the place, lights sparkled in windows and gardens were filled with extravagant displays. The darker winter nights were lit up by the excess fairy lights and Christmas cheer. Declan loved Christmas, but sometimes, he thought everyone went overboard.

The taxi pulled up at the bar before his thoughts could turn morose and dim his enthusiasm for meeting up with the crew. He thanked the driver, held his card up to the machine to pay and exited.

He could already hear the conversation and laughter coming from inside Crush, and no doubt from outside in the Garden Bar area. The hanging garlands on the front of the building showcasing the time of year as surely as anything else. Crush had been his go-to bar since it opened, and he'd made good friends with the manager, Tom. With it being a Saturday night, the bar was heaving, so he elbowed his way through the crowd towards the bar, slipping in between two people when he got there. The dark polished wood counter reflected the fairy lights twinkling on the shelves behind the bar.

Charlie, Josh and Analise were all behind the bar, filling drinks and chatting to the customers. Since the extension, the bar had grown in popularity, which was a good thing, but it meant less seating was available because the main room itself was the same size, something he was sure the manager would be rectifying soon.

Charlie reached him. "Hey, Dec. Do you want your usual?" When Declan nodded, Charlie continued, "How're things? It's panto season now, right?"

"Almost. We start performing next week."

"Ah, this is your pre-performance night out, is it?" Charlie grinned, glancing to the side when his boyfriend, Josh, squeezed past him. They had been together for around eighteen months despite the scandal surrounding their so-called taboo relationship. They brushed off the comments stating they were 'sick' for wanting their adopted brother. Their family and friends were fine with the development, so no one else mattered. At least, that's what Declan had told them several times.

"It sure is. I bet the rest of the crew are already around here somewhere." Declan stretched up, peering over people's heads to see if he could see any sign of them.

"I doubt they'll be outside. It's bloody cold tonight."

"I'd think it was about to snow if it wasn't only November. It's also probably why it seems so busy in here," Declan replied with a smile. "Bet Tom is over the moon with how well this place is doing."

"He is. I think he's got something up his sleeve, but he won't tell us what it is yet." Charlie laughed. "Always keeping secrets.

"Are you talking about me?" The man in question asked from behind Declan.

Declan turned his head to look over his shoulder. "Of course. Who else keeps secrets?" He had learned Tom enjoyed the banter when he wasn't stressed, and he certainly seemed relaxed enough that night. His black hair was longer than Declan had remembered seeing it for a while, the ends curling around his ears, and although he looked a little tired, his blue eyes were bright. He had some stubble, too, which was unlike the Tom Declan knew. Ginny was a good influence on him if she could get him to relax a lot more.

"I'm sure there are plenty of people, Dec." The corners of Tom's mouth twitched.

"Maybe, but around here, it's you." He pointed his finger at Tom when he slid in beside Declan after the previous occupant left. "How's Ginny? And the little one?"

"Both are good. I can't believe Kayleigh is going to be one soon. It's crazy how time flies." Tom shook his head.

"I know the feeling. I see it every day when I walk into the theatre, and I'm surrounded by teenagers." He laughed

"I am not a teenager!" a disgruntled voice piped up next to him.

Declan hadn't realised the neighbour from his other side had changed. "You might as well be one next to me," he grumbled to Micah, taking a swallow of the beer Charlie had placed before him.

"You wouldn't like it if I called you an old man, would you?" Micah replied.

Declan tilted his head in acknowledgement.

Tom patted his shoulder. "You'll outshine them all, no doubt. They'll be begging you for your knowledge soon enough." Tom chuckled, squeezing his shoulder. "I'll leave you to your evening. Make sure you pop in when it's less busy so we can have a proper catch-up."

"Sure thing, Tom. Give my love to your family." Declan turned back to Micah when Tom left. "Did you manage to get a table?"

Micah nodded and thumbed over his shoulder. "Yeah, we're over there."

"Does anyone need a refill before we leave the bar?"

"Nah, we've just had one. Gemma has been a star and keeps checking on us."

Declan nodded and grabbed his beer, letting his place at the bar be taken by someone else after a nod to Charlie. He weaved his way through the masses, following Micah until they reached a table overflowing with people.

"We might have to commandeer the Garden Bar at this rate," Declan mused.

"It might be an idea."

"Let me go and check whether the heaters are on out there."

Declan strode to the back door, slipping through it into the chilly night air, though not as chilly as it would have been without four heaters throwing out substantial warmth. There were two couples out there, meaning there would be plenty of room for them all. Rather than wading his way through the patrons again, he messaged Micah and sat down in the less noisy area, enjoying his beer and the less Christmassy décor. He wasn't a grinch by any stretch, but when you had to be festive for seven weeks in a row, the shine wore off.

Laughter and conversation spilled out the door when the theatre troupe exited the main bar area. Several of them pulled their coats closed, but none baulked at the change of location. He knew the newbies—what they call anyone who had only been there once or twice—quite well now, although Micah stood out because this was his third year. Don and Freddie were old-timers like him and had been playing in the pantomime for ten years or so, but both were younger than Declan was.

"I've let Gemma know where we are," Micah said, pulling up a chair next to him, their legs resting against each other.

He shifted in his seat, dragging his gaze from where their legs were joined to Micah's green eyes. A shiver went through Declan, which had nothing to do with the cold, and he frowned. What was all that about?

2

Micah

M icah had no idea how much he had drunk, but he knew it was getting late. He needed to grab some food before he threw up every drink he'd consumed that night.

Their party had thinned as the night wore on, leaving only the hardcore repeat offenders at their table. These were the people he had come to know during his two years at the theatre company, and the man sitting beside him meant more to him than Declan knew. Micah had never hidden the fact he was gay, and none of the crew had ever said anything against him, not even in jest, so he believed it wasn't a problem for them. He hoped, at least. But he was a silly man who had a crush on his straight friend. Talk about cliché.

The age gap didn't make any difference to Micah. He was attracted to whoever he was attracted to. As far as he was concerned, a guy could be forty years his senior and still be worthy of Micah's love. The straight aspect, though, was different.

Micah couldn't stop his gaze from returning to Declan time and time again. Eyes greedily drinking in the strong features, windblown raven-coloured hair speckled with grey, and a goatee he would love to feel dragging along his naked skin. However, he'd never seen any indication Declan was into men.

Clearing his throat, Micah tore his gaze away and focused on his drink. He needed to get over it. He'd seen Declan go home with women before. He knew he had no hope, but he couldn't do anything *except* hope anyway.

"I need to pee," Declan suddenly declared, standing abruptly and knocking his chair over. He stumbled towards the double doors and disappeared into the building.

Micah decided to grab another beer and followed in Declan's wake, heading to the bar instead of the bathroom. Josh smiled when Micah dropped onto a stool at the bar.

"I wasn't sure if you guys were still here," Josh said, grabbing a beer for Micah.

"Yeah, only the last few stragglers." At least, that was what he thought he said. Josh chuckled, so he must have said something right. "Don't you get fed up with Christmas lights?"

"Not really. I forget they're there for the most part."

Realising he needed a piss, too, Micah believed Declan should've had enough time to finish up and leave. He had no problem using the bathroom at the same time as Declan, but he knew his barriers were down, and he wasn't sure what would come out of his mouth if they were alone.

"Can you hold it for me while I go to the toilet?" he asked Josh, who nodded.

Managing to get his feet working, Micah drifted down the hall to the bathroom, his hand trailing along the wall to steady himself. Entering, his eyes locked on Declan, and he cursed silently.

"Everything alright?" Declan stared at him as he washed his hands.

Or maybe not so silently. "Yep." Micah stumbled to the urinals, fumbling to get his jeans undone and sighing when he emptied his bladder. Washing up after, he turned to leave, realising Declan was still there. "You okay?" Micah frowned and scrubbed at his face, trying to sober up.

Declan leaned against the wall, resting his head back. "I'm getting too old for this."

Micah couldn't believe they were back to that again. "You're not old, Declan." He came to stand in front of Declan, trying to gather his thoughts. If they were going to go through this again, he needed to concentrate.

Declan sighed. "I think this is going to be my last year, Micah," he whispered. Declan lifted his head to face him.

"Fuck that. You are the best one there, Declan. You can't leave." The bathroom spun a little, and Micah reached out a hand to steady himself on the wall. Instead, he ended up grabbing at Declan. Micah's gaze came to rest on his hand, which gripped Declan's shirt. He should let go, but he really couldn't. His fingers wouldn't open. He blamed the alcohol.

"Thank you, Micah. That means a lot."

Declan's voice wound around him, and Micah felt himself swaying forwards. His gaze lifted to Declan's, seeing resignation and sadness in his eyes. "No," he whispered before reaching up and pressing his mouth against Declan's.

He swiped his tongue over Declan's lips, then realising what he'd done, Micah pulled back, eyes wide and suddenly feeling extremely sober.

"Shit, sorry."

He released his grasp on the shirt and attempted to step back. He stopped when an arm slid around his waist and a hand cupped the back of his head. Barely having the chance to understand what was happening, Micah's eyes automatically closed when Declan's mouth met his, this time with more force. His back pressed against a wall, although how he got there, he had no idea because he was focused on the fact he had Declan's tongue in his mouth.

Micah encircled his hands around Declan's neck, returning the kiss and lifting onto his toes to get closer. He could feel Declan's hands roaming his sides and ass and shuddered with how hard his cock was. He thrust his hips forward, trying to gain some friction, and met with Declan's shaft, also rock solid. Micah rotated his hips, pressing and retreating, building their arousal higher.

All of a sudden, cold invaded where Declan had been pressed against him.

"What the fuck am I doing?" Declan muttered.

Micah stared at him, fingers resting against his own lips as he regained his breathing and equilibrium, which was difficult to do with the amount of alcohol in his system. "Dec—"

"I have to go." Declan turned around and slammed out of the bathroom, leaving Micah standing there.

"Fuck."

• • • ● • ● ● • •

Micah had written out so many texts to Declan in the four days since *the kiss*, but none of them had been sent. He didn't know what to say, and maybe, he was a little scared about what Declan's reply would be. There was also no answer Micah could give to the inevitable "Why did you kiss me?" question.

Today was the day he would see Declan in person. They had three days until the first performance, so they would be practising one section per day to ensure they had it all figured out. Micah's lips quirked at the memory of their last rehearsal. Hopefully, Declan's feet had sorted themselves out.

Wrapping up warm for his trek to the theatre—his roommate, Rae, wasn't there to give him a lift—he locked up and trudged along the path. The air was cold and brisk, but he walked faster to heat his limbs. The closer he got to the town centre, the more people he saw in heavy winter coats and hats, scurrying along, carrying multiple carrier bags loaded, no doubt, with presents.

Music drifted from the shops he passed, the universal sound of Christmastime all around him.

The theatre loomed ahead. The old stone building was three storeys high and had been around for decades; Micah had no idea how long exactly. Four columns were decorating the front with a huge arch housing the front door, which welcomed visitors but not staff. The theatre was not open yet; therefore, he had to enter through the side door located down a drafty alley between the buildings.

Entering the theatre, his heart pounded painfully, and his hands were clammy. He had no idea how to explain, but Micah knew he had to say something. Heading backstage, he smiled and greeted several of the cast and crew, asking after their families or how their weekend was, but he knew he was delaying the inevitable.

When he saw Declan on the stage, Micah paused and inhaled. He waited until Declan had finished performing the piece, then cleared his throat and stepped forward.

"Hey," Micah said hesitantly. "Can I talk to you?"

Declan glanced at him briefly before taking his gaze somewhere behind and walking past Micah as if he didn't exist. "Nope."

Micah raised his eyebrows, mouth gaping. Did Declan seriously brush him off? Chewing on his bottom lip, he realised Declan was *really* pissed off about what happened, but how was he going to fix things? Was Declan pissed off about the kiss or pissed off because Micah hadn't called?

"Micah! It's your turn!" Catherine, the choreographer, shouted at him from the wings opposite, and he jumped. She was a tiny thing, but her voice was not so small when it needed to be...which was always.

Glancing over at her, he waved his hands in a five-minute gesture and jogged to the changing rooms. Luckily, he only had to strip off his outerwear and change his shoes; the rest of his outfit was joggers and a t-shirt. They weren't using the outfits until the first performance now, not wanting any of them to get ripped or broken before the start.

Stepping onto the stage, Micah rolled his head on his neck, loosening himself up as much as possible. When the music started, he stood in place, pretending to be the snowman. The young boy, Alfie, began the motions of decorating him with a hat and scarf and 'coal,' which was black pompoms with sticky stuff on the back. When Micah wore his costume, Alfie would be sticking the coal onto the velcro to turn him into a decorated snowman as the scene progressed.

Micah found this part to be the hardest part of the whole show because he had to keep stone still for quite a long time. The director, Simon, had originally considered using a mannequin for this part but eventually chose to use a real person instead. "Less chance of the person falling than the mannequin," the director had said. Although Micah wasn't so sure it was true when he was inside a sweltering costume. They'd have to wait and see whether he ended up on the floor after performing several times a day.

When the music changed, it was his cue to get himself moving. The first time Micah had done this, he hadn't been able to move for a few minutes because he was so stiff, and after some discussion, they decided to have Micah move slowly, making it look like the snowman was getting his bearings, whereas he was getting his joints to move more freely before he had to run and jump around.

By the end of the first section, he was sweating and starving. He'd hardly seen anything of Declan, but that wasn't unusual because Micah only really saw him towards the end of the performance. The final section rehearsal was on Friday...when he'd have to properly face the guy.

Micah trudged to the changing room, intending to throw his stuff back on and not bother with a shower until he got home, but he stopped still when he saw Declan. Taking a quick look around to check no one else was in hearing distance, he walked towards Declan timidly as if he was approaching a fierce jungle cat.

"Can we please talk about what happened?" Micah said, voice low.

Declan spun around, gave Micah a once-over and turned back to his original position. "There's nothing to talk about."

Micah moved a step closer. "What do you mean there's nothing to talk about?"

"Nothing happened. Forget it." Declan shoved things into a bag, his movements hurried and rough.

"I don't understand, Dec." He placed a hand on Declan's back, smoothing it upwards, attempting to soothe him.

Declan whirled around, getting in Micah's face. "Forget. About. It. Nothing happened."

Micah took in Declan's flaring nose, heavy breathing, narrowed eyes and flushed skin. If it had been anyone else, Micah could have said the guy was aroused, but Declan did not sound pleased, and Micah didn't want to chance checking out his groin in case Declan got the wrong idea and laid him out flat.

Reaching behind him to grab the packed bag, Declan glared at him and stormed off.

Micah blew out a breath. The longer he stood there thinking over their interactions, the more annoyed Micah became. There was no need for Declan to speak to or ignore him as he had. All Declan had to say was it was a mistake, and it wouldn't happen again. But no. Declan had become all pissy about it instead. Who was the elder in this case? He didn't think it was Declan.

Pulling on his clothes per his original plan, Micah said goodbye to the people he passed as he left the theatre and headed towards home. He'd get another chance to see Declan tomorrow. Maybe the man would've calmed down a little by then.

· · • • ● • ● • ● • ● • · ·

Micah blinked when he opened the door of the apartment and saw boxes upon boxes of decorations with Rae standing in the middle of them all, tinsel draped around her neck.

"It looks like a Christmas shop barfed in here."

He removed his coat, hat, scarf and gloves, leaving them near the entry radiator to warm for when he next needed them. Navigating around the boxes, he came to a stop next to Rae and raised his eyebrows at her.

"Dad dropped by with some of their excess decorations. I'd mentioned when I last spoke to them that we didn't have much." Her forehead creased as she looked around. "I didn't expect this, though."

Micah laughed. "Of course, you did. When have your parents ever done things by halves? This is probably a quarter of what they wanted to bring but knew it wouldn't fit in the apartment."

He weaved around the track again, heading to the kitchen to grab a tea. With how much coffee he dealt with at the coffee shop, he had taken to drinking tea instead. The smell of coffee often made him think he was at work. When his tea was brewed, he grabbed a can of coke for Rae and trailed through the towers again, carefully sitting on the only space left on the sofa.

"Thanks," Rae said when he handed her the drink. "Do you not want me to decorate?"

Rae was confident in most aspects of her life. Coming from a family who didn't have to worry about money had made her a bull in a china shop sometimes. But when it came to living together, she made a conscious effort not to brush off his opinions, which he was grateful for.

"It's fine. I'm hardly here anyway."

"I won't put up too much."
Micah snorted. He'd believe that when he saw it.

3

Declan

"**D**eclan! Micah! What the hell are you playing at?" Simon shouted at them. The director usually had a lot of patience, but he had stopped them more times than Declan could count that afternoon. "What the hell happened between last week and now? You both had this down. Why are you fumbling around like newborn foals? If you don't get your heads out of your asses, you'll be out of a job! The performances start tomorrow!" He emphasised the final word before turning around and rubbing his hands over his hair. "Take a break, but I want you back in ten minutes."

Declan hustled to the break area, grabbing a fresh bottle of water and guzzling several mouthfuls. He was fucking exhausted already, but most of it was to do with a tall, slender guy with porcelain skin and red, curly hair. Since their...moment last weekend, Declan had only slept in short bursts, being woken by dreams he didn't want to remember, then unable to sleep for several hours afterwards unless he'd jacked off.

He couldn't help but remember the way Micah smelled, like gingerbread and musk; the sounds Micah made when their tongues twined; the hardness of Micah's cock against his own. Said cock perked up at the images flowing through his brain, and Declan inhaled deeply, trying to focus his thoughts elsewhere.

He knew they needed to discuss it, but Declan was afraid it would make it more real rather than a drunken hazy dream he could pretend didn't happen, even if only in his brain on the odd occasion it switched off.

Micah entered the break room, and Declan threw his empty bottle in the bin and exited, hearing a huff behind him but ignoring it. He strode to the stage, ready—but maybe not quite willing—to go through it again, hopefully without second-guessing where he put his hands while they were dancing.

That was the problem. Before, Declan hadn't had to worry about it because, although Micah was gay, Declan had no reason to think about where his hands went. Micah knew Declan was straight; therefore, he wasn't worried about Micah thinking Declan was trying it on with him. It was only dancing, after all.

Now they'd had...that moment, Declan was concerned Micah would get the wrong idea. He knew it was stupid, but he couldn't help it. So, their dancing had been a mess of fumbling hands and fingers, which was all Declan's fault.

"Right, you two. Are you ready to try again?"

Declan nodded and got into position. This section of the show was where the snowman introduced the boy to Father Christmas. The dialogue was no problem at all, but then the boy stepped away, and the snowman and Father Christmas began a dance before all the other snowmen joined in for the party. They had to bow to each other, hold opposite hands, dance up and down the stage before helping each other to do a kind of air kick around the area. Once they'd done it, they danced a short tango sequence to make the audience laugh before the snowman pushed Father Christmas away and pretended to become shy. That section was more aimed at the grown-ups.

"Well, it was significantly better than what you have been doing today, but it's not up to par compared to last week. What's going on? Have you two had a lover's tiff?" Simon chuckled.

"No!" Declan hissed. "I'm tired, is all."

Simon rubbed his face. "If you're tired after four days of rest, Dec, what are you going to be like by the end of the complete run?" He sighed. "Get some rest. I'd like you back for one more go through in three hours, then we'll let the chips lie where they fall." He turned and walked away.

Declan felt his face get warm as his insecurities about ageing out of the theatre came back to the forefront of his mind.

"Don't you dare," Micah growled, coming to stand in front of Declan. Declan was so surprised, he stayed still. "You are not getting old. Get that thought right out of your head. The theatre keeps you young forever."

Micah gave a half-smile, which Declan returned. Turning to walk away, he felt Micah fall into step beside him.

"Talk to me, Dec. Please."

Declan gritted his teeth, the brief humour they'd shared disappearing. "There's nothing to talk about."

They both entered the changing room, where several people were in the process of changing costumes. Declan was glad their conversation could not be continued, so he grabbed his stuff and left as soon as he was ready. He would have enough time to grab a bite to eat, have a bath and give himself a stern talking to before heading back to the theatre. By that point, he should be back to normal. He hoped.

• • • ❷ • ❷ • • •

He wasn't—later that afternoon *or* the following day.

The first performance began, and although it was good, it was *not* perfect, which bugged the hell out of Declan. A sucker for perfection, when it was him dragging behind, he was pissed. And because he was pissed, it made things worse.

By the end of the two initial shows, he stormed out of the theatre and drove home, deciding he would drown his sorrows. He had six days to get his act together before the next performance—he was lucky the initial show was for kids, and it would only make it funnier if they stumbled.

Tequila became his friend that night. The following morning, it became his enemy. Nursing a hangover, he sat in front of the TV, watching something mindless while his thoughts bounced around his bruised and battered brain. He was so confused.

Never had he ever had feelings or inclinations towards a man. He had been heterosexual for all his life. But all it took was one kiss—and he refused to acknowledge more than once that it was an amazing kiss—and he second-guessed everything. Declan also ignored a lot of what his brain and body told him. Unable to figure out what was happening to him, he chose to forget about it.

The problem was, every time he thought about Micah, his stomach fluttered, and his breathing increased. Every time he saw Micah, his heart pounded, and his palms became sweaty. Every time he closed his eyes and slept, he dreamed about Micah. There was no escaping him, and it made Declan grouchy. So grouchy, he refused to decorate his house, much to his sister's amusement.

"I know you don't hate Christmas, Dec, so what's got your knickers in a twist?" Maggie asked with a grin, draping herself across an armchair in his living room. She was the quintessential Scot with flaming red hair and the green eyes of their grandparents. How it had missed Declan, they had no idea. There had been many jokes in the past of Declan being the postman's son, much to the laughter of his parents.

"Nothing. It just seems like Christmas gets earlier every year," he grumbled.

"Bullshit. What's happened?"

Declan debated about what to say. He knew he'd get nothing except the truth from her, but did he want to face what she might have to say?

"Let me work it through myself, Maggie. At least, for now."

She stared at him for a few moments, then nodded. "For now."

They spent the evening catching up and watching action movies. He relaxed with the knowledge she wouldn't push him until she believed he needed to be...which was probably tomorrow. He inwardly rolled his eyes, knowing his sister as well as he knew himself.

• • • • • • • • • • •

"What do you want to drink, Dec?" Catherine shouted to him.

"Just a beer, please."

True to their routine, the whole cast celebrated the start of the season with drinks two days before the next performance. Declan had almost declined but decided he needed to stay being part of the cast; otherwise, they would begin to see him differently...unapproachable, maybe. He'd seen it happen before. Older cast members started to step back, and the younger ones thought the older ones were too good to be with them. He didn't want to be that person.

Managing to avoid Micah that evening had worked, except for the odd glance across the table at each other. Each time it happened, Micah had a frown on his face. Declan ignored the pang in his chest at the expression.

When it came time for the next show to start, Declan felt a little better about the situation. If he stopped thinking about it, he believed he would be able to carry on as normal.

That night, the show was a huge success. Declan was pleased his idea had worked and made a note to do the same thing each time. He gathered his things and, being the last to leave the changing room, switched off all the lights. There was a crew who would shut everything down and lock up, so he didn't need to.

He stepped out into the frigid winter night and saw Micah standing in front of the theatre, arms crossed, shivering as he hopped from foot to foot. Declan was about to walk off when his helpful personality refused to let him leave without checking up with him.

"Everything okay?"

His words startled Micah because he jumped a foot in the air and swore like a sailor. "Jesus, Declan. You scared the shit out of me."

Declan withheld his smile. "Sorry. Are you alright?"

Micah checked his phone, shoulders slumping. "Yeah. I'll be fine." He smiled, though it didn't reach his eyes.

"Where's your ride?" Declan knew Micah's roommate picked him up after most performances because he didn't have a car and the buses didn't run his way.

Micah was silent. He sighed. "No idea."

Declan closed his eyes and shook his head minutely. "Come on. Let me take you home."

"No, it's fine. I'll call a taxi," Micah mumbled.

"Micah." He waited until Micah looked at him. "Let me take you home."

Micah stared at him, biting his bottom lip, and Declan could do nothing to stop his internal—and external—reaction to the sight. He swallowed hard and turned away, heading towards the car park, expecting Micah to follow. Unable to hear any footsteps, Declan glanced over his shoulder to see Micah a few paces behind, studying the ground. Declan knew this was a bad idea, especially if Micah decided to get into the discussion he'd wanted them to have. It was frowned upon to throw people out of a car when it was moving. Didn't mean Declan wouldn't do it.

They climbed into Declan's car, and Declan asked for Micah's address, flicking the heaters to full warmth. "Can you direct me, or do I need to get the route?"

"I can show you where to go," Micah replied. "Thank you for this."

"No problem."

They started off, and apart from Micah's directions, there was silence until Micah asked, "Why do you keep ignoring me?"

Declan had no idea how he could reply to the question without making Micah feel like crap, so he ignored it. "Are you seeing your family on Christmas Day?"

Sighing, Micah linked his fingers together in his lap and stared out of the window. "Yes. They're driving down to see me this year, and we're going to a restaurant for dinner."

"Sounds nice. No having to cook for you, then." Declan gave him a small smile, hoping to begin to build bridges between them.

"What about you?" Micah turned in his seat slightly, his back to the door.

"Well, my sister is cooking for both of us, which is good because it means I don't have to cook either."

Declan turned onto Micah's road and parked at the kerb in front of his building.

"Thank you, Dec. I appreciate it."

Micah pulled the handle to open the door, and suddenly Declan didn't want him to leave without giving him something. Some sort of explanation.

"I'm trying to figure myself out. It's not easy when you're forty-five and thought everything was cut and dry."

Declan didn't look at Micah while he made his confession, but he heard the whispered, "Thank you," when Micah climbed out and shut the door behind him.

It wasn't much, but maybe Micah would understand what Declan hadn't voiced.

When Declan arrived home, he put some leftovers in the microwave and heated them, eating in front of a documentary on the TV. It was all white noise to his thoughts. He needed to figure out what was going on in his head, but he couldn't fathom what he was really feeling compared to what he believed he *should* be feeling, although he knew there was no *should* to this. He could feel however he wanted to feel, but it was difficult to change the way he'd always believed himself to be.

As he'd said to Micah, how could he change forty-five years' worth of believing he was straight? But then again, how could he not challenge his belief when forced to acknowledge his reaction to Micah.

Putting his plate down, he laid on the sofa, staring at the ceiling. For the first time, he truly looked inside himself while he thought about their kiss. And for the second time, it shook him to his core.

4

Micah

Micah couldn't believe what Declan had acknowledged. He understood what Declan had been saying and finally realised he had been pushing Declan quicker than the man was ready to face the changes. If Declan *was* ready to face the changes. He might decide to stay as he was, which was his right.

Hoping Declan would eventually make a choice Micah would be content with, he could do nothing more than give Declan space even as much as he wanted to climb him like a tree.

It wasn't too difficult a thing to do because he stayed away from the guy while the show was running unless they had a scene together. Outside of the theatre, he worked as a barista, and at that time of year, he was always asked to take more shifts, which he did if they didn't interfere with the performances. This meant him joining the cast and crew when they went out was severely restricted.

So, all in all, he was able to give Declan the space Micah believed the other man wanted.

What Micah didn't like was the thought that once the pantomime was over, he wouldn't see Declan regularly anymore unless they were cast in another show together. But Declan was acting like this was his final hurrah, so to speak.

A few days before the long run of performances up to Christmas, Micah was standing making coffees for the patrons of the café, side-eyeing the clock and listening to a repeated Christmas album over the speakers. He had over three hours before he finished work, but that day had been difficult. He hadn't wanted to get out of bed but knew he couldn't let the coffee shop staff down. Unfortunately, though, he thought he might be coming down with something, and the sooner he could get home and take something for it, the quicker he'd recover. It was the worst time to get ill, and he hoped he was wrong.

"A large cappuccino, please."

Micah swung his gaze over his shoulder so fast, he could have given himself whiplash. Declan stood at the counter with a small smile. Turning back to the drink he was making, Micah's thoughts whirled. He didn't remember Declan ever visiting the café before, but it didn't mean he never had.

Tina nudged his shoulder and passed him a piece of paper with a wink.

Do you have a break coming up?

Micah concentrated on the drink and passed it over to the customer with a smile before returning to make Declan's drink. Once it was finished, he carried it to the counter and slid it onto the tray along with his reply to the answered question.

"What was all that about?" Tina whispered when there was a break in the customers.

"He's a friend from the theatre." Micah fought to keep his voice neutral and his face from becoming a beacon.

"Uh-huh. Sure."

"He is, actually. He plays Father Christmas."

Tine raised her eyebrows. "Seriously?"

Micah nodded and turned back to his station, waiting for the next order. By the time his break arrived, half an hour later, he was ready for it. Not only because Declan was waiting for him but because he was knackered. He made up two more cappuccinos and carried them to the table where Declan sat, weaving around the square tables and obstacle course involving shopping bags, pushchairs and umbrellas.

"You didn't have to—" Declan started.

"I know, but I thought it might give us an excuse to stay at the table for a bit longer. I only have twenty minutes, though."

"That's fine." Declan hesitated, his forehead creasing. "Are you okay?"

Micah sighed. "I think I'm coming down with something. I need to get home, which I can do in just over two hours, and I can rest. I will not get ill while the performances are happening." He grinned.

"Break a leg."

Declan chuckled, and Micah enjoyed the sound he'd not heard aimed at him for a while. They used to laugh and joke a lot before.

They fell silent, the noises of the café surrounding them: the clink of the cups, mumbles of conversation, the squeak of shoes on the linoleum floor, the thump of the door opening and closing.

"Look, Micah..." Declan fiddled with the napkin in front of him. "I would—"

All of a sudden, Micah's head began to pound, his eyes went blurry, and his stomach rolled. He pressed a hand to his forehead while battling back nausea. He inhaled and exhaled slowly, trying to let the feeling pass. When he became aware of his surroundings again, he was being cradled in someone's arms as they carried him somewhere.

"It's okay, Micah. I've got you."

His eyes closed, and he succumbed.

The next time he blearily blinked open his eyes, his whole body ached, despite the softness of the bed beneath him. He groaned, and a shadow fell over him, placing a cool cloth to his forehead.

"You're alright, Micah."

He rolled his head slowly to the side until Declan came into view. "What're you doing?" he muttered, mouth feeling like sandpaper.

"I'm keeping an eye on you." Declan paused. "Is that okay?"

Micah had no idea. He could barely keep his eyes open. The scent surrounding him was comforting, though he couldn't figure out why.

"Rest."

Micah closed his eyes again.

When Micah opened his eyes again, they felt scratchy, and the room was dark apart from a small lamp on his bedside table. It had been turned to face away from him, he assumed to keep it from straining his eyes. Something was placed at his lips, and he automatically opened his mouth, distantly realising it was a straw. He swallowed the cool liquid and fell asleep again.

Soft movement roused him, and he lay warm and content, listening. When he heard the fabric rustling, he carefully rolled his head on the pillow to see what it was. He raised his eyebrows when he saw Declan sitting in a chair next to his bed. He wore joggers and a t-shirt, which Micah couldn't remember seeing him wear outside of training sessions. His hair was mussed as if he'd run his hands through it repeatedly.

"How are you feeling?" Declan asked, leaning forward and resting his forearms on his knees.

Micah's gaze shot to Declan's, not bothered about being found staring.

"Like I've been hit by a truck."

Declan chuckled deep and low. "I bet."

"What time is it?"

"Shouldn't you be asking what day it is?" Declan smirked. "It's Friday. Roughly three in the morning."

"What?" Micah whispered. "How...?"

Declan nodded. "You've been out of it for two days. The doctor says it's the flu."

"A doctor came to see me?" How had he missed it? He was usually a light sleeper.

He nodded again. "Your temperature spiked quite high, and I was concerned." Declan appeared shy in his declaration, his focus dropping to the floor.

"Have you been here the whole time?" Micah tried to sit upright, but Declan stood, lifting him carefully to a seated position with pillows supporting him. That small movement wore him out.

He sat back in his seat and said, "I have. Except when I nipped home to get a few changes of clothes."

"Where's Rae?" It didn't surprise him that Rae would pass this onto someone else.

"She's been in and out. She's been working."

Micah shook his head, knowing Rae was pulling the wool over Declan's eyes. Rae never worked. She didn't have to. "I'm sorry you've had to stay here. You can head out if you like. I should be fine now." Micah didn't want Declan to go, but he must be shattered. Despite having been out of it, Micah felt comfortable with Declan there.

"I'm fine. Managed to get some reading in that I've been meaning to do. Don't get much chance at this time of year."

"Oh, god! The show!"

"Calm down."

"What am I going to do. I need to get better. Let me get up." He flung the covers back, swinging his legs over the edge of the bed, preparing to stand.

"Micah!" At Declan's shout, Micah paused before his feet hit the floor. "You're not going anywhere. We both have Saturday and Sunday off now. The director has called in the understudies for our shows. Now get back into bed."

Micah slumped back against the pillows, groaning while he returned his legs to their previous position. "I'm sorry, Declan. I'm a bloody nuisance."

"No, you're not. You're ill. You can't help it."

"I can't believe I have the flu. What did the café say?" He ran a hand over his face. "They're short-staffed already without me being off, too."

"Your manager is a mother hen if you haven't noticed." Declan's mouth twitched, and his eyes gleamed when he spoke about the mother of all mothers.

"She is. She's also the best person I know."

Declan nodded. "I saw that. She told me to tell you that you are not allowed back at work until New Year."

"But...she hasn't got enough staff!"

"That's where Rae is. She's taken over your job for now."

Micah's mouth gaped. "What is this alternate universe? Now I know I'm ill and not thinking clearly."

Declan smiled. "She said you'd never believe it."

"I don't think Rae has worked a day in her life. Her parents are filthy rich, and she's just never had to." She was an awesome person, except when it came to taking care of ill people. She hated it.

"From what Rae told me, she's been doing okay. A few little mishaps here and there but mostly fine." The twinkle in Declan's eye made Micah think something had happened, but he was too tired to ask about it. Declan leaned forward again and helped Micah to lay down. "Rest some more. Rae will fill you in later."

• • • • • • • • • •

By Sunday morning, Micah felt much better. He was eating better, sleeping better and had been able to stay awake the whole of

Saturday. How that day went influenced whether he'd be able to perform on Monday. He hoped he could. He missed it.

Declan had been around him for most of the time he'd been ill, including most of the day before, and Micah hoped he wouldn't fall ill himself. Declan had finally been persuaded to go home and sleep, but he'd only agreed to it if he could come back on Sunday to check on him. Micah had agreed for selfish reasons. He wanted to spend more time with him. Although Micah did say that Declan wasn't allowed to come back until after lunch.

Rae had returned the previous evening with dark circles under her eyes, so he hadn't spoken to her more than to say thank you and goodnight. He planned to discuss the job with her that day because he knew he wasn't scheduled to work, so in theory, she wasn't either. When Declan had told him what she'd done for Micah, he'd been blown away. No one had ever done something like that for him before.

He stood, making sure his legs were steady before shuffling towards the kitchen for tea. He'd had enough water to last him a lifetime and was in sore need of caffeine. As the kettle boiled, he popped some bread in the toaster and fetched mugs for him and Rae. No doubt, when the scent of coffee spread through the house, she'd be seeking it out. He smiled. She was predictable when it came to some things.

"Morning," she mumbled, trailing into the kitchen and dropping onto a chair before resting her head on her arms, her long brown hair tumbling around her in a cascade of curls.

"Good morning." Micah placed a slice of toast in front of her and filled a mug with coffee granules and hot water. He set the mug on the table with the milk beside it. "How are you today?"

Rae groaned. "Knackered."

Micah snorted. "I bet." He plated his toast and carried it and his mug to the table, sitting opposite his roommate. "Thank you, Rae."

She lifted her head, and he saw tired but bright eyes gaze back at him. "You're very welcome, Micah. And thank you for the drink and food."

They ate in silence, but when they'd finished, Micah asked, "How have you been doing?"

Rae shook her head, finishing her mouthful. "Crazy. I never realised what you had to put up with."

Micah waved her away. "It's life. At least you didn't have to cover the pantomime."

They locked gazes for a few seconds before they burst out laughing. There was no way she would have been able to cover for him. She was the world's worst actor.

"You'd have been fired in less than a minute if I had," Rae said once she'd regained her breath.

"Well, I'm hoping I can get back to it tomorrow. I've missed everyone." Micah drank some more of his coffee, closing his eyes when the taste hit his mouth.

"Are you sure you'll be well enough? I don't want you to go overboard and get sick again. I can't do this working thing for-ever." She smirked.

Micah chuckled. "I'll take it as easy as I can."

"Well, I'm keeping on with your shifts at the café until New Year. You only have to concentrate on the pantomime."

"You don't have to—"

"Non-negotiable." She smiled, a sparkle in her grey eyes. "I'm actually quite enjoying it." Rae rested her elbows on the table, lifting her mug closer and watching him over the top. "I might ask for a position after you go back. See if they want me to help out."

Micah raised his eyebrows. "But you just said...I didn't think you'd enjoy it so much."

"Me neither."

They spent the morning together, catching up on their lives like they'd not managed to for the past week. Rae told him stories of some things that had happened at the café, and Micah enlightened her to some of the gossip surrounding the staff. Rae also mentioned his parents had called while Rae was at work, and Declan had fielded the conversation, so Rae had no idea what was said. He made a mental note to ask Declan about it.

5

Declan

Declan had hardly slept again. Even though he'd been able to relax knowing Micah was on the mend. He would doze off easily enough, but visions of a fevered and confused Micah kept invading his dreams, making him wake up in a sweat. And not the good kind of sweat, either. When Micah's fever had spiked and wouldn't lower, Declan had panicked and wasn't sure what to do. He'd called his sister, who'd told him to ring for a doctor. Luckily, one had been able to visit that same day. After prescribing some medicine Rae had nipped out to get, the doctor had explained what to do to help, outside of giving the medicine.

Even now, his heart jumped at the thought of how ill Micah had looked. He'd hardly woken in two days, and Declan had worried about what would've happened if he or Rae had not been there.

When he had visited Micah the previous afternoon, after being told to stay away until lunch, Declan had seen Micah was doing much better. He thought it was too soon for him to start back at the pantomime as Micah had been determined to that day, but it wasn't his job to decide for Micah. Though, Declan would've loved to be able to. It was yet another thing that bugged him about their situation—his need to help Micah as more than a friend.

The whole time Declan had spent with Micah, even when the other man had been delirious, he'd been trying to work through his feelings. He'd finally come to the conclusion he thought Micah was attractive, which for someone who had not noticed any guys before, was one hell of an acknowledgement. He'd replayed the kiss a million times, getting off to it many times too.

He was so confused.

Micah had arrived at the theatre, looking pale but in high spirits and eager to catch up with everyone. He received several hugs and pats on the back when he walked through the changing room. When he reached Declan, Micah gripped his forearm, squeezing gently and gifting him with a smile. Declan's breath caught in his lungs, but Micah was already turning to his costume.

Declan continued dressing in his first costume of the evening, hoping things were going to go well.

Two and a half hours later, he trudged into the changing room with several other cast members, laughing and joking despite being shattered. He had left all the previous animosity behind and had fun, which showed in the performance. Simon had caught him before he entered the dressing room, telling him the performance had been the best one yet.

They now had an hour and a half until the second performance of the day. He wanted to check in with Micah and see how he was holding up.

As soon as the thought crossed his mind, Micah entered, looking flushed, sweaty and tired but happy, if the smile on his face was anything to go by. Declan understood the rush. It was a similar feeling to what he had every time he stepped off the stage, knowing the performance had been great. Declan hadn't been able to see every scene Micah had done, but he had appeared to be managing.

"How are you feeling?" Declan asked when Micah stepped over to their area. He stopped himself from reaching out to check Micah's forehead.

Micah grinned at him. "Knackered but alive."

Declan quirked his mouth. "Yeah, we don't want a dead snow-man parading around the stage. It might frighten the kids," he quipped.

Micah laughed, and the sound lifted Declan's heart, such a contrast to the previous week.

"One more to go. Do you think you'll be okay?" Declan tilted his head, gaze roaming over Micah to figure out the truth about his health.

"Yeah. I'm going to grab a bite to eat, then catch a short nap before this next one." Micah smirked. "I don't want someone telling me I'm too tired to perform."

Declan's gaze rose to Micah's eyes, watching them sparkle, heat blazing low in Declan's stomach. Micah's choice of words did not bring up images of the pantomime but of other types of performing. Declan cleared his throat and turned back to his clothes.

"Good. You need your rest." His voice sounded hoarse even to his own ears, and a shiver raced down his spine.

The following performance went off without a hitch, too, and the cast closed the night with a large cheer for Micah's recovery.

· · ● ● ● · ● ● · ● · ●

Being two of the main characters in the show, Declan and Micah were often chosen for the final part of the performance, where they allowed four children from the audience to come on stage and have a 'chat' with them both. That day was no exception. Dressed as Santa, Declan grabbed a microphone and strode back on stage, Micah following behind him.

"Have you all had a good time?" he shouted to the audience. A half-hearted yell came back, as always. He grinned and glanced at

Micah. "Well, that was rubbish." He turned back to the audience and repeated, "I said, have you all had a good time?" A louder response came then. "That's better."

"Father Christmas?"

"Yes, Snowman."

"I think we have some visitors."

They both looked to either side of the stage, beckoning with their hands for the children to join them. They lined the four children up, facing towards the audience.

Declan knelt next to the first child. "And what is your name?" he asked.

"Tara," a small voice said.

"Hello, Tara. What would you like for Christmas?"

"A doll's house."

"Ooh, sounds nice. Have you been good this year?"

"Yes, Santa."

Declan grinned and hugged her.

Micah asked similar questions to the child closest to him, Neil, who wanted a race car and faltered when asked if he had been good, earning a chuckle from the audience.

Declan focused on his next child, Ava, who wanted a whole bookcase full of books and had been the best girl in the whole world—three guesses as to who might be joining their ranks one day.

Micah shuffled forward to see the final child.

"What's your name?

"Janie."

Declan glanced across at the girl, who he hadn't paid attention to before, and realised it was his friends' daughter, which meant they were in the audience somewhere. Janie wanted a bike for Christmas and had been super good for her dads. Everyone said, "Aww," when she answered.

After the children had been reseated with their grown-ups, they all had a singsong before Declan and Micah said goodbye.

As soon as they were backstage, they stripped off their face-coverings, breathing a sigh of relief at the fresh air reaching their sweat-slicked skin. Declan glanced over at Micah and saw a drop of sweat rolling down the side of his face and had the uncanny need to follow it with his tongue. He cleared his throat and looked away.

"I'm going to quickly get changed and see if I can catch my friends before they leave."

"Oh, are your friends here?"

"Yeah. Do you know the last girl? Janie? She's my friends' daughter. I've not seen them for a while."

"Get going then." Micah shoved his shoulder, laughing.

Declan grinned and hurried up. He exited the cast area and glanced around the milling crowd in the foyer of the theatre, most probably grabbing another drink for the road or using the toilets before their journey home.

He couldn't see his friends until he heard his name and saw them standing near the exit. He weaved his way towards them.

"Hi." He gave Sean and Asher a hug, then leaned down and wrapped his arms around Janie. "Hey, princess. How are you?"

Declan had met Sean and Asher at Crush through Tom. Sean had been the architect involved in the creation of the Garden Bar last year, and Asher was a childminder. There was a whole host of people who were friends and often met up at Crush. Declan had met most if not all of them.

"I'm good. Did you see me on stage?"

"I did. You were so good, Janie." He flicked the end of her nose, making her scrunch it up and laugh. At six, she was a gem.

Declan stood once more, smiling at the dads. "How have you been? I've not seen you around Crush for a while."

Sean grinned. "We've been there, although probably not as much as usual. We did celebrate a couple of birthdays this last weekend, along with another event." He bit his lip and glanced at Asher, who smiled.

"Uncle Sean gave Uncle Asher a ring," Janie pronounced.

They all cracked up, and Declan gave them another hug each, congratulating them.

"Here, he is." Asher crouched down when another young boy joined their group, waddling his way towards Asher's out-stretched arms. Asher picked him up, blowing a raspberry on his cheek.

"Sorry, it took so long. There was a queue."

Declan turned to the young boy's father, Zak, and held out his hand. "Hey, nice to see you."

"You, too. Are you joining us?" Zak asked, eyebrows raised.

"Where are you heading?"

"To our house," Asher declared. "You're welcome to come for a drink or two."

Declan thought about it and decided they might be able to help him figure out what was going on in his life at that moment. "That would be great, thanks."

Half an hour later, they were seated in Asher's large living room, each holding a beer while Janie and Dane played with the bricks. Declan could see Asher's childminding skills had rubbed off on Janie.

"What's going on with you, Declan? As you said earlier, we've not caught up for a while."

Declan took a breath. "Actually, there's something I'd like to ask your opinion on if you don't mind. It's a little personal and out of my comfort zone, but I need a sounding board."

"Sure," Sean said, leaning forward.

Declan fiddled with the label on the beer bottle, collecting his thoughts. "I've always thought I was straight. I'm trying to figure out if it's changed." He didn't want to look at any of them to see their reactions. "A guy kissed me a few weeks ago, and I responded before pulling away in shock. Admittedly," he felt himself flush, "I didn't do well with it and was a complete..." he glanced at the kids before mouthing the word "ass." "But things have changed, and I don't know if I'm..." He stalled.

"Feeling things that are real or not?" Asher supplied.

"I suppose, yeah."

"When you think about the guy, what initial feelings go through you?" Sean asked.

"He's hot." Declan slapped a hand over his mouth, eyes widening at his words.

Asher, Sean and Zak chuckled.

"I'd say you need to spend some time with this guy. See if sparks fly. Talk to him, though. Explain how you feel because if you decide not to go ahead with it, you don't want to hurt him. Especially if he's already your friend," Sean said.

"I'm...scared," he whispered.

Janie came over and climbed into his lap, cuddling into him. "When I'm scared," she whispered, "I get huggles."

Declan closed his eyes and pressed a kiss to her head. "Thank you, Janie."

They changed the subject and ended up ordering pizza for a late dinner once the kids were settled into bed. Zak had planned to wake Dane when it was time to leave, but Sean and Asher told him there was enough room for them to stay. Enough room for Declan, too, if he wanted to.

Declan thanked them but declined, knowing he needed his morning routine at home to feel centred for the performances the following day. Declan had great fun catching up over the food, and after a few hours, he bid goodbye with promises to call them if he needed anything.

Once he'd arrived home, it didn't take long for the good cheer of the evening to wane. There was no time like the present to try and figure out his thoughts, especially since he was unlikely to be able to sleep right away. The fifteen-year age difference didn't bother Declan as much as he thought it would. Although he felt his age when he was around the other actors at the theatre, with Micah, he didn't feel it. They had things in common despite their age, and he felt...content when he was with Micah. That was the only word he could find to explain how he felt around him.

Excluding his sexual orientation for the moment, Declan had no issues with being in a relationship and working with Micah at the theatre. There had been many relationships, both successful and unsuccessful, throughout his years, and he didn't see a problem with it.

His sexual orientation was a different matter. He couldn't ever remember having feelings for guys in the past, but it didn't mean he couldn't. He wasn't afraid of being gay or bisexual or whatever he might identify as, but he liked to *know*. It sounded stupid, but he liked having a label he could identify with and explain. He didn't like being in limbo.

When Micah had been ill, Declan had been worried about him. Really worried. He'd hardly slept the whole time, scared he'd wake to find Micah gone.

Declan's eyes shot open at the thought, and he stared into the darkness, tasting his emotions, testing their reality. If those words hadn't made everything crystal clear, nothing would.

Smiling, he snuggled into the covers. He had plans to make. He needed things in place before he explained everything to Micah, and he needed to do some research.

6

Micah

Micah thought he'd been throwing out signals to Declan about his interest, but they had either not been understood or had been ignored. He didn't know how much more obvious he could be without throwing the man against a wall and kissing the hell out of him.

That didn't work last time, so he doubted it would again.

The final performance before Christmas ended, and although he usually joined the crew for the Christmas Eve celebration—they were all about celebrating every little thing—he couldn't work up the energy to meet up with them. That was until Declan grabbed hold of his hand and practically dragged him to his car and deposited him in Crush with the rest of the cast.

Micah wouldn't be staying long, and he certainly would not be drinking. He hadn't completely recovered from the flu, so he wanted to be careful.

The manager of Crush had set aside a large area for them, obviously knowing they were coming, and Micah gratefully dropped into a chair with a sigh.

"Sorry, Micah. Do you want me to take you home instead? I thought some time out would be good, but if you're too tired, I can take you home," Declan said from beside him.

Micah glanced at him, seeing the strain around his eyes, which deepened the lines on his face. "Nah, I'm good. Just a relief to sit down." He chuckled.

Declan smiled. "There is that. Well, when you want to leave, let me know."

I'll stay here as long as you do, Micah thought, studying Declan's profile.

After they had their drinks, conversation started up around them. Micah asked Declan about his friends and how he knew so many people.

Declan laughed. "When you get to be my age, you'll have plenty of people you know and call friend, but you might not see them often. If they are good friends, though, you'll find you can start where you left off."

Micah would've loved that, but he didn't think his list of friends would grow much. Apart from the crew at the theatre, he didn't socialise much. They spoke about their Christmas plans again and what they were doing for New Year. Neither of them had plans because they were performing both New Year's Eve and New Year's Day, so drinking was out of the question.

Declan appeared to be more relaxed around him now their kiss had been pushed aside. Their performances had returned to their pre-kiss quality, but Micah missed their back and forth. It had returned a little, but nothing close to where it had been before it all happened, and Micah was sorry for it. He carried on normally, trying not to feel upset about the situation, and despite wanting to kiss Declan goodbye when he dropped Micah off at home, he refrained and waved instead.

The following morning dawned cold and misty, the chill enough to warn of the possibility of snow, although Micah doubted it. He had no idea when the last time there had been snow on Christmas Day. He wrapped up warm and waited quietly for his parents to arrive to pick him up; Rae had already left for her parents' house.

"Merry Christmas, Mum, Dad," he said, climbing in the back of their car.

"Merry Christmas, Micah," his mum replied. His dad said nothing, only started driving.

"We booked Romano's. Hope that's okay."

His parents were not into traditional Christmas food like turkey or stuffing. They preferred the 'finer' things in life; therefore, their choice of venue was not a surprise. Not that Micah minded. He loved the food they served at Romano's, but he would've preferred, for once, to have a roast dinner with all the trimmings.

He loved his parents dearly, and they had taken his news of being gay without a hitch in their relationship, but sometimes he wished...

Anyway, they wouldn't be staying long. After spending a couple of hours with him, they would drop him back home before driving onwards to his brother's house, where they would stay for dinner.

He was never invited to join them. He and Reg had never been close—the ten-year age gap too much for them to find any solid compatible interests. Reg was an investment banker, like their dad, whereas Micah was a lowly actor and barista. Micah was lucky his parents had agreed to pay for his Performing Arts degree, although they often said it was a waste of money.

Micah didn't think so.

Therefore, despite the fact his parents didn't want to be with him at Christmas, he sucked it up and let them pretend for a couple of hours. After, he returned home and turned on a Christmas movie and snuggled under a blanket on the sofa until Rae joined him a couple of hours later. Then, the fun began.

· • • ● ●• ● ● ● •·

The remainder of the performances passed by without a hitch. Their final show ended with a standing ovation with flowers given out to the director, writer, choreographer and others, too. The whole cast and crew were buzzing with excitement while they dressed in their street clothes and left the theatre for the bar. The final celebration of the season was about to start.

As usual, the bar had sectioned off an area for them—Micah wished he knew who did it for them—and the bartender Charlie brought a round of beers for everyone.

Micah found himself sat next to Declan again, who was drinking water because he was the designated driver. It had become a routine thing now, them sitting together, and they began chatting about what the next show was going to be. It couldn't be Aladdin or Cinderella because they'd be done the previous two years, and whereas Declan believed it would be Jack and the Beanstalk, Micah chose Beauty and the Beast. A few other members chipped in their thoughts. None of them would find out until March when the writer would disclose what had been chosen and who would be directing and supporting the show.

The evening wore on, and Micah became more relaxed as the alcohol flowed. He had completely recovered from the flu, thankfully. They had been served food at some point, which had soaked up some of the booze, but Micah was feeling no pain. He felt bad about what happened with Declan, which is why he thought it was a good time to broach the subject, especially since he probably wouldn't see Declan until March.

"Hey, Dec. I'm really sorry about what happened before. I didn't mean anything by it, and I didn't mean to cause problems." Micah's focus remained on the drink in his hand.

Declan lifted Micah's chin until their gazes locked. "I'm not sorry."

Micah frowned. "What do you mean? You were so angry."

"I was confused," Declan countered. His thumb brushed at Micah's chin. "I'm not confused anymore."

"About wha—"

Micah didn't get to finish his sentence before his mouth was covered by Declan's. His shock morphed into a moan when their tongues tangled together, and Micah gripped the front of Declan's shirt. He had no idea how long they kissed before the sound of whistling and shouting invaded his brain. Micah pulled away, glancing around the table at his theatre family, whose faces had a mixture of shock, joy and laughter.

He grinned but tucked his face into Declan's neck, hiding. He felt Declan chuckle, and Declan wrapped his arms around Micah, hauling him close.

The rest of the evening was spent trying to come to terms with a sober Declan claiming him in front of everyone, Declan being gay or bi or whatever, and Micah getting his Christmas wish—a little late but better than never.

• • • ● • ● • • •

When Declan dropped Micah home, Micah invited him in. He wasn't expecting them to progress their relationship that night, but he wanted to talk to Declan and make sure they were on the same page. The kiss had been a shock to his system, but it hadn't been the only kiss they'd shared that night. Several times throughout the evening, Declan had claimed his lips, and his hands had been on him regularly, whether holding his hand or with an arm around him.

It had been wonderful, but Micah needed something else: reassurance that he wasn't an experiment.

"Would you like a drink?" Micah asked.

"I'm alright, thanks."

Micah grabbed himself a glass of water, draining half of it straight away. He needed to clear his head if they were going to have a conversation. He refilled his glass to the top and headed into the living room where Declan was waiting.

Micah dropped onto the opposite side of the sofa to where Declan was, curling his legs under him so he could face Declan.

Declan raised his eyebrows. "Why so far away?"

"We need to talk."

"Sounds ominous."

Micah lifted the corners of his mouth. "Nah, just trying to figure out what we're doing."

Declan nodded. "I can understand that." He rubbed a hand across his mouth. "When you first kissed me, I had forty-five years of believing I was straight. It came as a shock to me that I not only kissed you back, but I enjoyed it."

"I'm sorry."

"No! Don't be sorry. *I'm* sorry for being so angry afterwards." Declan reached across the space and rested his hand on Micah's. "I didn't understand what I was feeling. Everything was a jumbled-up mess, and I blamed you when you did nothing wrong."

"Except kiss a straight guy." Micah grinned.

"It's not against the law as far as I know." Declan smirked. "I had already started to come around to the idea when you fell sick. The fear that went through me when you collapsed at the café that day..." Declan shook his head, eyes staring straight ahead. "Even then, I couldn't come out and say something because I didn't understand myself. I've done a lot of soul-searching these past few weeks."

"Thank you for taking care of me." Micah moved closer, snuggling into Declan's side, the other man's arm pulling him closer.

"I couldn't leave you. My heart wouldn't allow me to walk away."

Micah lifted his head and puckered his lips, asking for a kiss. Declan snickered and lowered his mouth, fusing their lips for a short time. When Declan pulled back, Micah whimpered at the loss.

Declan continued his story, "I spoke with my friends, trying to figure things out, and they were amazing. I shocked them with my announcement, but they helped me. I didn't want what happened last time to happen again. So, while it killed me to do it, I waited. Until tonight. Now, we don't have to worry about messing up a performance."

Micah chuckled and stared up at the man he had fallen for many months ago, despite Declan's off-limits status.

"I can't promise what tomorrow will bring, Micah, but what I can promise is to communicate with you every step of the way."

"That's all I can ask."

"And you don't mind being with an old man?" Declan's eyes twinkled.

Micah backhanded his shoulder. "You're not old. You're perfect. For me."

"So, are we doing this?" Declan raised his eyebrows, and Micah could see the veiled worry in his features.

"Yeah, we're definitely doing this thing." Micah straddled Declan and lowered his mouth, sealing their pact with a kiss.

• • • ● • ● • • • •

Micah finished clearing up the plates and stacking them in the dishwasher. Declan had cooked; therefore, it was his turn to tidy up. He had no idea where Declan had wandered off to because he had done so as soon as dinner had finished, saying he needed to do something.

He was feeling a lot more at home in Declan's house after a month together. Though he'd not moved in, they were always at either his house or Declan's and hardly ever spent a night apart now. He smiled, remembering their first night together. Declan had been so nervous, but Micah hadn't planned to get Declan to fuck him straight away. Instead, he'd introduced him to the pleasures of frotting, and by the time evening had fallen, they'd both come multiple times.

It began a nightly routine, which had included blow jobs when Micah had sunk to his knees a few days after their first sexual experience. Declan had been blown away—literally—by it and had laid in stunned silence for several minutes afterwards, finally explaining none of his ex's had ever made him feel like that. Micah had preened at the compliment.

Never wanting Declan to feel pressured into intercourse, Micah had been content continuing their routine. Declan had been concerned he wouldn't like sucking Micah off, but when Micah had swiped his fingers through their combined come and licked it off, Declan had attacked his mouth, leaving no area untouched. As soon as he'd finished, he'd slid down Micah's body and swallowed him whole.

Apparently, Declan had no gag reflex. How about that?

"Micah?" Declan called from upstairs.

He dried his hands on the towel and hung it back up before heading to the stairs and jogging up two at a time. Anyone would think he was eager. Micah chuckled at himself. He was always eager to see Declan.

"Where are you?" he asked, heading towards the bedroom.

"Bedroom."

He saw Declan stood beside the bed with his back to him, and he walked over and slid his arms around his waist, pressing his cheek into his shoulder blades. "What's up?" He felt Declan take a deep breath.

"I want to fuck you," he whispered.

Micah grinned and held him tighter. "Fine by me."

Declan twisted in his arms, expression taut, eyes a little wild. "I've done some research, but..." He licked his lips, and Micah saw his Adam's apple bob when he swallowed. "Can you teach me?"

Understanding how much it had taken for Declan to say the words, Micah rose onto his tiptoes and pressed a kiss to Declan's lips. "I'd love to."

Declan's face relaxed, and he gave a small smile, leaning down to capture Micah's mouth. They'd realised they both loved kissing, especially the soul-destroying, mind-blowing, hard and heavy ones that left them gasping for air. When they surfaced, they were breathing heavily and trembling.

"Let's get undressed," Micah said, sliding his hands down and under Declan's t-shirt and retracing his steps against Declan's skin until he could pull it off over his head. Micah pressed a kiss to the exposed skin, licking a path between his nipples when Declan cupped his head and groaned.

Tilting his head back, Micah looked at Declan, whose pupils had blown wide. "Get on the bed, Micah."

7

Declan

Declan's hands were trembling as he removed his jeans, watching Micah scramble onto the bed and roll onto his back. When Micah's eyes widened at Declan standing in only his briefs, he quickly removed his trousers and threw them over the edge of the bed, leaving him encased in black briefs that did nothing to hide how aroused he was.

Licking his lips, Declan knelt on the bottom of the bed, crawling slowly towards Micah, his eyes focused on the man who had come to mean so much. He pressed a kiss to the underside of the covered dick and carried on up until he blanketed Micah and their shafts met.

"You always feel so fucking good, Dec."

Declan said nothing but covered Micah's mouth with his own, licking inside immediately and tasting him. Their hips moved, sliding their cocks against each other. Micah bit Declan's lower lip, holding onto it as he pulled away until he groaned and let go.

Declan kissed down Micah's neck to his nipples, circling one before fluttering his tongue over the nub repeatedly. Micah groaned and lifted his hips, gripping Declan's hair. He moved his mouth over to the other nipple, giving it the same treatment before making his way down Micah's abdomen to the happy trail pointing to where his destination was.

Sliding his fingers underneath the waistband of the briefs, Declan lifted them over the steel shaft before yanking them off completely and throwing them over his shoulders. Micah settled his legs on either side of him again, and the magnificent cock was his for the taking.

When he'd first thought about putting a dick in his mouth, Declan had scrunched his nose up at the idea until he'd tasted Micah's come on his lips. As soon as he had, he'd slid down and sucked Micah until the other man had come again, swallowing every drop, and the rest, they say, is history.

Eyeing his treat, Declan licked at the tip, collecting the escaped precome and groaning in delight.

Micah nudged his arm with something cold, and he opened his eyes, seeing the lube. Declan took the tube, unclicking the lid while he concentrated on the head of Micah's cock. He used his tongue to flick at the underside, his hands busy getting the lube onto his fingers, then he lifted off with a final lick.

Spreading his legs wider, Micah smiled at him when Declan lifted his gaze to check on him. "I'm good. So fucking go-ood," Micah moaned as Declan circled a finger against his entrance. "That feels amazing. Press a little harder each time, and you should feel me relaxing and letting you in," Micah breathed.

Watching Micah for any indication he was hurting him, Declan continued his ministrations, pushing a fingertip into him when he opened. Declan had never seen this except for on the porn he'd watched to figure out the logistics. It was mesmerising to see Micah's ass open for him. His finger slid in and withdrew several times, going further in each time. Micah's mouth gaped wide, and he was breathing heavily.

"Now, two."

Declan concentrated on his movements, his second finger joining the first. It seemed incredibly tight, the channel squeezing against the intrusion, but he could push them in. Micah's hands were gripping the sheets, and he was trembling, but no words telling Declan to stop.

"Three," Micah's voice was hoarse, directing Declan while in the throes of arousal.

When Declan pushed three fingers into Micah's ass, he bit his own lip at the sight. The hole was stretched around them, fluttering and clenching while he pressed forward and back, forward and back until Micah's head was thrashing against the pillow.

"I need you! Dec. You. Now."

Declan removed his fingers and lifted onto his knees. He grabbed the lube and slicked his bare cock, both having decided to forgo condoms after they'd been tested and found to be clear.

"Ready?" he asked, bracing himself over Micah.

"God, yes. Fuck me, Dec."

He held his cock at Micah's entrance, feeling the heat on the tip before he pressed forward. The resistance felt insurmountable until he pushed harder and slid through the tight ring. They both groaned when Declan thrust forward, settling deep inside Micah. When his balls rested against Micah's ass, Declan paused, dropping to his elbows.

"You're so tight and hot. Jesus, Micah." He rested his forehead against Micah's, eyes closed as he revelled in how it felt to be inside him.

"Please, fuck, Dec. Move."

Declan opened his eyes and lifted his head after pressing a kiss to Micah's mouth and braced himself on his hands again. Watching where they were joined, he withdrew until he could feel only the tip inside and thrust forward, groaning when he was encased in heat once more.

"Oh god, Micah, you feel amazing."

When his control broke, Declan drove forward, their skin slapping together while he fucked Micah as hard as the other man asked for.

"Fuck, yeah!" Micah's voice was hoarse, and he gripped Declan's forearms. "I'm coming!"

Declan's hips stuttered when he felt Micah come around his cock, his channel squeezing him tightly. Declan came with a groan, sliding back and forth until he was too sensitive. He withdrew and dropped on top of Micah.

"You're trying to kill me."

"What's the matter, old man? Can't keep up with me?"

"I'll give you old man, kiddo."

Declan bit Micah's lip, then it turned into a kiss. When he pulled away, they stared at each other.

"Thank you," Declan said.

"For what?"

"For not giving up on me. For teaching me how to love. How to love you."

Micah's eyes misted, realising what Declan was saying. "I love you, too." He paused. "Even though declarations of love during sex don't count."

"Shut up."

"Make me."

Declan growled and showed him how much of an old man he was *not*.

$$\bullet \, \bullet \, \bullet \, \bullet \, \bullet \, \bullet \, \bullet \, \bullet \, \bullet \, \bullet$$

There's more to come from the Just a Little Crush world. Read on for a teaser of A Special Love.

And you'll receive a free short story, exclusive content and updates if you sign up to my newsletter.

A Special Love Teaser

Rory

"Have you seen Beethoven? And the ones after it?" Rory asked while he tried to keep a golden retriever still so Heath could work on its cut paw. The poor thing had stepped on something on their walk that morning, and Rory had immediately taken him to the clinic. Nothing to do with being able to see Heath again or anything, naturally.

Heath gave him a droll look, then refocused on Baxter. "Who hasn't seen them? I prefer Turner and Hooch, though."

"Yeah, that was good. I don't think there are many dog films I haven't seen. Even the animated ones."

"A movie buff, are you?" Heath said as he cleaned the wound, making the dog flinch and whine before covering it with a bandage.

"Definitely. It's what I do when I don't work." Rory paused. "Which isn't very often, I admit." He laughed.

"In which case, would you like to go to the cinema with me?"

Rory gazed at Heath while he finished working, wishing the guy would look at him so he could get an idea of whether it was a date or just a night out with a friend. When the silence stretched out, he answered, "Yeah, that would be great. Do you know what's on at the minute?" He was glad his voice sounded semi-normal.

"To be honest, I don't have a clue. Let me wash up, then I can check my phone."

Rory studied the man's actions while he cuddled with Baxter, allowing the dog to lick his face as Rory scratched behind his ears.

"All righty, then."

Heath pulled his phone from his pocket and rested back against the counter across from Rory. With Heath focusing on his phone, it gave Rory time to examine his features. The usually closely cropped hair had grown out some since he first met Heath back in September, and it was a style that looked good on him. Anything would suit him. Heath's freckles, while still there, were less visible now that the sun had stopped darkening them.

"Here are the choices." Heath came to stand next to him and tilted the screen so Rory could see. "It all depends on when you'd like to go, I suppose?" Heath reached up to scratch his jaw, their shoulders brushing.

Rory tried to concentrate on the screen, but it was difficult. "Um...why don't you choose? I'm happy to watch pretty much anything."

"Okay, as you seem to trust me so much, I'm going to surprise you." Heath smirked. "What about after work on Friday?"

Rory's gaze roamed over Heath's face, seeing his eyes crinkling with mirth. "Fine by me."

"Great. I'll swing by to pick you up about six-thirty."

"No, don't come out of your way. I'll meet you there."

Rory saw Heath's eyes tighten, but he grinned and nodded. "Okay."

There was a knock at the door, and Elaine popped her head in. Rory had come to know her through their phone conversations, but it had been nice to finally put a face to a name.

"Mr Holland is here with Beatrice."

"Thanks, Elaine. We've just finished."

Elaine's eyes flicked from Rory to Heath, and a small smile played on her lips. "I'm sure."

She closed the door behind her, and Rory frowned at Heath. "What was that about?"

Heath glanced away and walked around to the other side of the table. "No idea."

Rory raised his eyebrows but left it alone. "Right. I better get going then. Come on, Baxter. Let's see if Carlton has burned the place down yet."

They both laughed, and Rory exited the treatment room. He stopped by reception to sign the paperwork and pay for the appointment, but Elaine waved him off.

"Heath said he'd sort your bill later."

Rory nodded and bid goodbye, carrying Baxter to the car. Unable to believe he was going out with Heath in three days, he smiled the entire journey back to the shelter.

"Wow, what's *that* smile for?" Emma said as he walked in the door.

"What smile?" Rory tried to dial back his grin but found he couldn't.

Emma chuckled. "*That* smile." She pointed at his face. "The cat has got the cream smile. Who made you so happy?"

"That would be the vet, I bet," Carlton stated, walking into the foyer.

"Well, aren't you a poet," Rory shot back, heading for the back.

Unfortunately, they both followed when he carried Baxter to his kennel and settled him in with some fresh water and a treat.

"Did he ask you out? Did you ask him out? Did you make out?" Emma babbled, keeping up with him when he strode towards the building once more.

"Emma! Please!" Rory stopped, Emma crashing into the back of him. "Fine." He faced them with his hands on his hips. "Heath asked me to go to the cinema with him on Friday night."

"Yeah!" Emma and Carlton fist bumped.

"It's not a date."

They both frowned at him. "But you just said—" Carlton started.

"I know. But I don't think it's a date. I think we're just going as friends." Rory could hear the uncertainty in his own tone.

Carlton stepped forward. "It would surprise me if this wasn't a date, Rory."

"How do I know?" Carlton and Emma shared a look, which Rory decoded to mean they had no idea. "Don't worry about it. I'll just see how it goes." He drifted off with a wave and went to his office. Paperwork was calling. He wasn't hiding at all.

Grab the book here : https://books2read.com/aspeciallove

Books by Elouise East

Illuminate Matchmaking
Ignite
Blaze
Kindle
Scorch

Club Royal
Royal Firsts
Rogue Royal
Secretive Royal
Grieving Royal
Disowned Royal
Trained Royal
Awakened Royal
Commanding Royal

Boys, Daddies, Snuggles & More
Need Him
Trust Him

Daddy
Love Me, Daddy
Soothe Me, Daddy

ELOUISE EAST

Spoil Me, Daddy
The Complete Daddy Series

Love in Flames
Out of the Frying Pan
Smokescreen
Breathing Fire
Love in Flames Collection

Crush
Love Conquers
Instant Desire
Primary Seduction
Deep Down
A Crush for Christmas
Life Support
Covert Strength
Love Scene
Lawful Attraction
Crush Collection Volume 1
Crush Collection Volume 2
Crush Collection Volume 3

Just A Little Crush
First Kiss
He's Behind You
A Special Love
Three Thirds
Sweet Truths

Standalone
Treehouse Whispers
Star-Crossed

Protecting the Thief
Sizzling Chauffeur

Elouise R East (taboo)
Dark & Divergent
Forbidden Temptation
Too Many Secrets

Collide
When Fantasies Collide
When Dreams Collide
When Pleasures Collide
When Cravings Collide

About Elouise East

Elouise East writes sweet and steamy connections in gay romance. She also touches on taboo stories under the name Elouise R East.

Books that tell the stories where friendship and family are the focal point - be it blood family or chosen - are very important to her. That's why she includes a variety of personalities, talents, ages, situations and abilities as she believes a story or character needs. She wants her characters to be real, to be relatable, to be free to have whatever views they tell her they have. And trust her, most of the time, she does not have *any* say in the matter!

Her characters come to life on the page for her as well as her readers. Their stories unfold in front of her as she writes, and she has very little input into how they want to be shown. Just like real life, the lives of her characters change with every choice, every interaction and every conversation. And she wouldn't have it any other way.

She writes books that are emotionally realistic, even if liberties are taken with other aspects of the stories. She doesn't know any other way to write. It comes from deep inside.

Who is she? A single parent to two children living in the UK. An avid reader who still tries to devour every book she can get her hands on. A student of learning about any subject that takes her fancy. An author of books she would read herself. And a romantic at heart who loves anything cheesy.

Who's joining her on her journey?

www.ingramcontent.com/pod-product-compliance
Lightning Source LLC
Chambersburg PA
CBHW030810190726
48285CB00003B/1113